Looking for Luna

written by **Tim Myers**

illustrated by **Mike Reed**

Marshall Cavendish Children

Text copyright © 2009 by Tim Myers
Illustrations copyright © 2009 by Mike Reed
Marshall Cavendish Corporation, 99 White Plains Road, Tarrytown, NY 10591
www.marshallcavendish.us/kids
Library of Congress Cataloging-in-Publication Data

Myers, Tim (Tim Brian)
 Looking for Luna / by Tim Myers ; illustrated by Mike Reed.
   p. cm.
 Summary: On a walk outdoors to locate their "soft-stepping, shining-eyed,
milk-lapping" cat, a father and child enjoy watching other felines tumbling in
the grass, creeping through flowers, climbing trees, and batting moths.
 ISBN 978-0-7614-5564-6
 [1. Stories in rhyme. 2. Cats—Fiction. 3. Lost and found possessions—Fiction.]
I. Reed, Mike, 1951- ill. II. Title.
 PZ8.3.M99537Lo 2009
 [E]—dc22
                    2008029399

The illustrations were rendered in Corel Painter using
a Wacom digital drawing pad. After the images were
drawn with traditional pencil and paper, they were
scanned by the artist and painted.

Book design by Vera Soki
Editor: Margery Cuyler

Printed in China
First edition
1 3 5 6 4 2

mc Marshall Cavendish
Children

To Margery Cuyler, not only a great editor,
but a wonderful writer, too—and fun to work with besides!
How lucky can a guy get?
—T.M.

To Jane, Alex, and Joe
—M.R.

We're after a cat,
a soft-stepping cat,
I'm walking with Dad and we're after a cat.
With me out in front and Dad close behind,
there's a wandering kitty we need to find.

We're searching the walkways,
scanning the streets,
peeking in places where cats like to meet,
I'm walking with Dad on sneaky feet,
    we're after a cat,
      a cat.

The first we see is black and white,
skittish and kittenish, frozen with fright.
But as I look, he bolts away—
when all I wanted to do was play!

Across the flowerbed, over the lawn,
dust in the air from his steps when he's gone.

I love watching cats, and searching is fun—
but I shake my head: It's not that one.

We turn a corner and then spot two:
one white with eyes of china blue,
one gold and tan, a tawny fighter
who stalks the white, pretends to bite her.

They tumble together, bunched on the lawn—
then suddenly stop, roll over, and yawn.

I love watching cats, it's totally true—
but I shake my head: It isn't these two.

We pass a rickety wooden house,
where a yellow cat's just caught a mouse,
a cat we rarely see, who creeps
through canna lilies, pauses, leaps
up to the top of the garden wall,
then shadows away like mist in fall.

I love watching cats—I always will.
But I shake my head, and we're searching still.

We gaze above us and then we see
an amber cat in a maple tree
who bats a moth right out of the air,
then shakes his thick and shining hair.

He turns to go when he sees us come,
but scornful, slow, too proud to run.

We stop in shade to take a breather;
I shake my head: Not that one either.

We're after a cat,
a milk-lapping cat,
I'm walking with Dad and we're after a cat.

We're looking ahead, we're looking behind,
in the oleanders and tamarack pines,
we're after a cat,
a cat.

Then all stretched out for a morning nap
is an amber-and-white, who wakes when I clap.
The sleepyhead opens one gold eye,
stands and trots to a tree nearby,

leans against it with outstretched paws,
rakes the bark to sharpen her claws.

I love watching cats, grown ones and kits—
but I shake my head: This isn't it.

Then suddenly we see the one
who says *Hello* each time we come,
dark tiger-stripes against her gray,
a fog-gray tail that gently sways,
a cat who stands without a fuss,
looks and smiles right back at us.

We found the cat! Imagine that!
This is the one—our own dear cat!
This is Luna, who ran away.
I want her back at home, to play!

And so, to lure her to our house,
I start to squeak her small toy mouse . . .

and she leaps into my arms, then purrs,
and I look down in those eyes of hers,
and we head for home to spend the day
with nothing to do but run and play!

That is…till Luna roams again,
and we start to miss our fog-gray friend . . .

until the next time Dad and I
go after a cat,
a beautiful cat,
searching the sidewalks, dodging the gnats,
happy to hunt among houses and flats
for a soft-stepping, shining-eyed, milk-lapping cat,
after a cat . . .

. . . a cat.